A NOTE T[O PARENTS]

MW01047726

Congratulations on choosing the best in educational materials for your child. By selecting top-quality McGraw-Hill products, you can be assured that the concepts used in our books will reinforce and enhance the skills that are being taught in classrooms nationwide.

And what better way to get young readers excited than with Mercer Mayer's Little Critter, a character loved by children everywhere? Our First Readers offer simple and engaging stories about Little Critter that children can read on their own. Each level incorporates reading skills, colorful illustrations, and challenging activities.

Level 1 – The stories are simple and use repetitive language. Illustrations are highly supportive.
Level 2 - The stories begin to grow in complexity. Language is still repetitive, but it is mixed with more challenging vocabulary.
Level 3 - The stories are more complex. Sentences are longer and more varied.

To help your child make the most of this book, look at the first few pictures in the story and discuss what is happening. Ask your child to predict where the story is going. Then, once your child has read the story, have him or her review the word list and do the activities. This will reinforce vocabulary words from the story and build reading comprehension.

You are your child's first and most influential teacher. No one knows your child the way you do. Tailor your time together to reinforce a newly acquired skill or to overcome a temporary stumbling block. Praise your child's progress and ideas, take delight in his or her imagination, and most of all, enjoy your time together!

McGraw-Hill
Children's Publishing

A Division of The **McGraw·Hill** Companies

Send all inquiries to:
McGraw-Hill Children's Publishing
8787 Orion Place
Columbus, OH 43240-4027

Printed in the United States of America.

1-57768-827-9

Library of Congress Cataloging-in-Publication Data is on file with the publisher.

1 2 3 4 5 6 7 8 9 10 PHXBK 07 06 05 04 03 02

 A Big Tuna Trading Company, LLC/J. R. Sansevere Book

FIRST READERS

Level **1**   Grades **PreK–K**

COUNTRY FAIR

by Mercer Mayer

McGraw-Hill Children's Publishing

Columbus, Ohio

I love going to the fair!

I can ride the ferris wheel.
It looks big.

I can hear tractors.
They sound loud.

I can pet horses.
They feel soft.

11

I can smell cotton candy.
It smells sweet.

I can eat popcorn.

It tastes salty.

I can win a teddy bear.
I feel happy.

17

Word List

Read each word in the lists below. Then, find it in the story. Now, make up a new sentence using the word. Say your sentence out loud.

Words I Know	Challenge Words
can	ferris wheel
ride	tractors
looks	sound
eat	horses
win	cotton candy
happy	popcorn

Mixed-Up Letters

These capital letters are mixed-up. Point to each letter and say its name. On a separate sheet of paper, write the letters in the correct order.

A M C N E

D G U F W

J K Z Q B

X O T H Y

P I L

R S V

Words and Letters

Read the story again. Touch each word with your finger as you read. Then come back to this page and answer the questions below.

How many words are on page 8?

Which words on page 6 have 5 letters?

Which word on page 10 has only 1 letter?

What is the 3rd word on page 14?

Challenge: How many words are in the whole story? Do not count the words in the pictures.

The Five Senses

These are the five senses. They help you to understand what is going on in the world around you. Point to each picture. Then point to the sense word that goes with it.

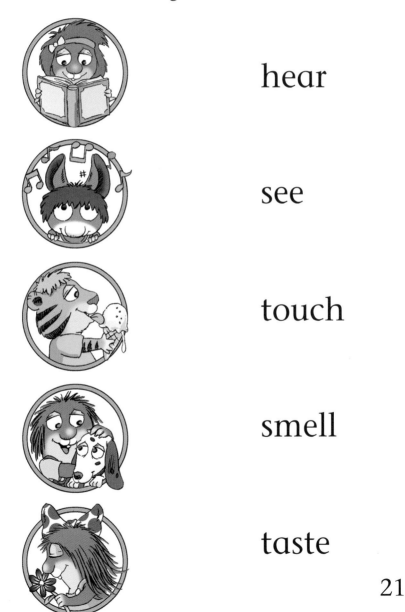

hear

see

touch

smell

taste

It Makes Sense

Little Critter and Little Sister are having fun at the fair. Point to all the things they can taste. Then point to all the things they can smell.

What can they touch, see, and hear?

What can the pig and frog taste?

What Happened?

A lot happened at the fair. Try to answer the questions below without looking back at the story. If you need help, use the page numbers to find the answers.

What looked big? (page 6)

What sounded loud? (page 8)

What felt soft? (page 10)

What smelled sweet? (page 12)

What tasted salty? (page 14)

Answer Key

page 19
Mixed-Up Letters

A B C D E
F G H I J
K L M N O
P Q R S T
U V W
X Y Z

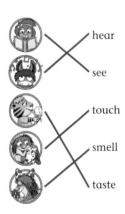

page 20
Words and Letters

How many words are on page 8? 7

Which words on page 6 have 5 letters? wheel, looks

Which word on page 10 has only 1 letter? I

What is the 3rd word on page 14? eat

Challenge: How many words are 53
in the whole story?

page 21
The Five Senses

hear

see

touch

smell

taste

page 22
It Makes Sense

Little Critter and Little Sister can taste:	popcorn
They can smell:	popcorn
They can touch:	popcorn, each other, the popcorn box, the drink cup, straw, the pig and frog
They can see:	the pig, the frog, popcorn and popcorn box, the drink cup, straw, each other
They can hear:	crunching popcorn, the pig drinking, the frog's tongue
Pig and frog can taste:	The pig can taste the drink. The frog can taste popcorn.

page 23
What Happened?

What looked big? (page 6) the ferris wheel

What sounded loud? (page 8) tractors

What felt soft? (page 10) horses

What smelled sweet? (page 12) cotton candy

What tasted salty? (page 14) popcorn

24